Wallpaper

To my friends who celebrated with me during my happiest moments
and held me together during my darkest hours. With much love — Thao

Owlkids Books acknowledges the financial support of the Canada Council
for the Arts, the Ontario Arts Council, the Government of Canada through
the Canada Book Fund (CBF) and the Government of Ontario through
the Ontario Media Development Corporation's Book Initiative for our
publishing activities.

Published in Canada by
Owlkids Books Inc.
10 Lower Spadina Avenue
Toronto, ON M5V 2Z2

Published in the United States by
Owlkids Books Inc.
1700 Fourth Street
Berkeley, CA 94710

Library and Archives Canada cataloguing in Publication

Lam, Thao, artist
    Wallpaper / by Thao Lam.

ISBN 978-1-77147-283-8 (hardcover)

    I. Title.

PS8623.A466W35 2018   jC813'.6   C2017-903890-7

Library of Congress Control Number: 2017943554

The artwork in this book was rendered in paper collage.
Edited by Debbie Rogosin and Karen Li
Designed by Claudia Dávila

ONTARIO ARTS COUNCIL
CONSEIL DES ARTS DE L'ONTARIO
an Ontario government agency
un organisme du gouvernement de l'Ontario

Canada Council
for the Arts
Conseil des Arts
du Canada

Canadä

Manufactured in Shenzhen, Guangdong, China, in
October 2017, by WKT Co. Ltd.
Job #17CB1229

A   B   C   D   E   F

Owl kids Publisher of Chirp, chickaDEE and OWL
www.owlkidsbooks.com

Owlkids Books is a division of **Bayard** CANADA

Wallpaper

by Thao Lam

Owlkids Books

blah-blah

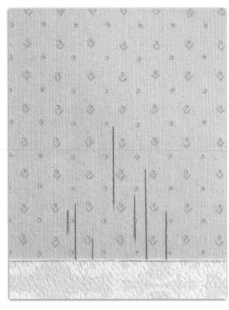

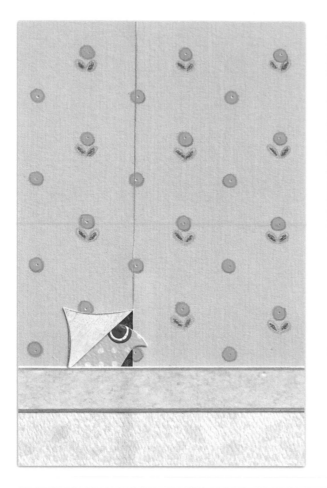

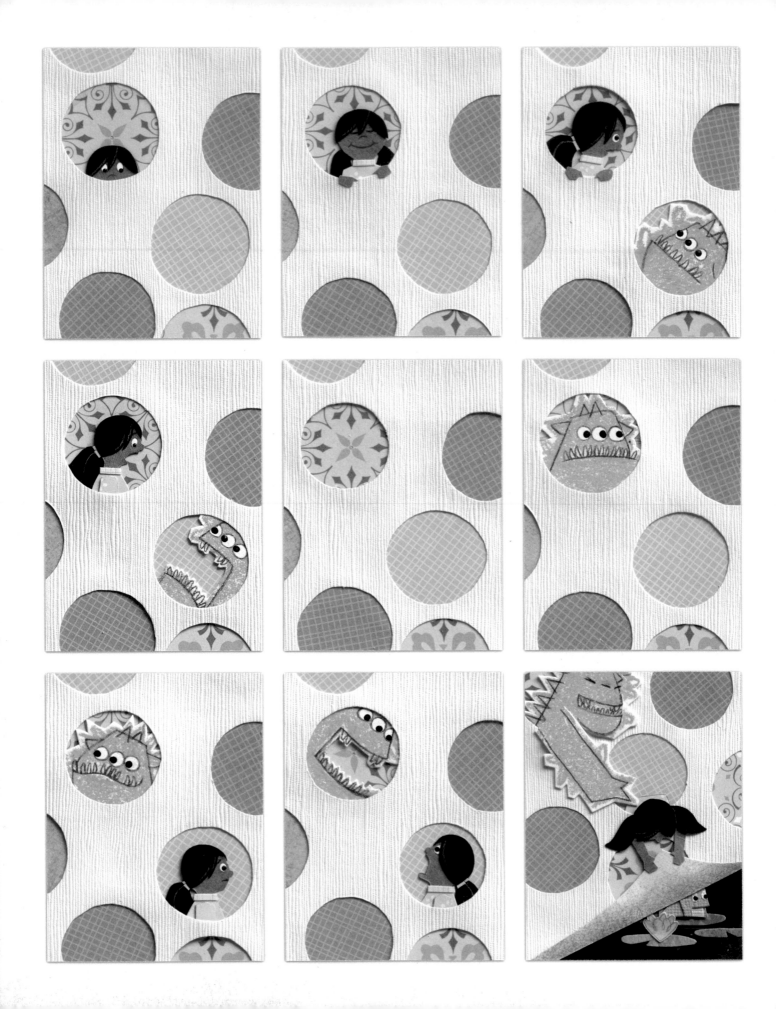

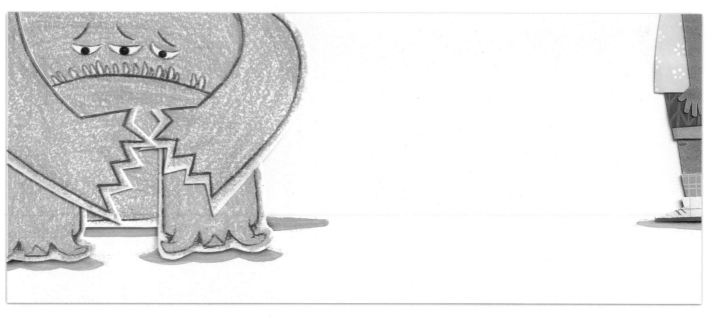
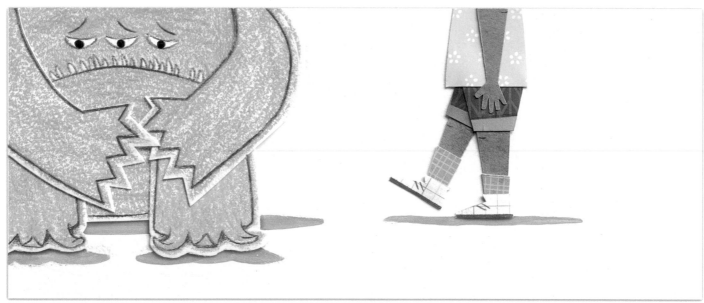

Hello.

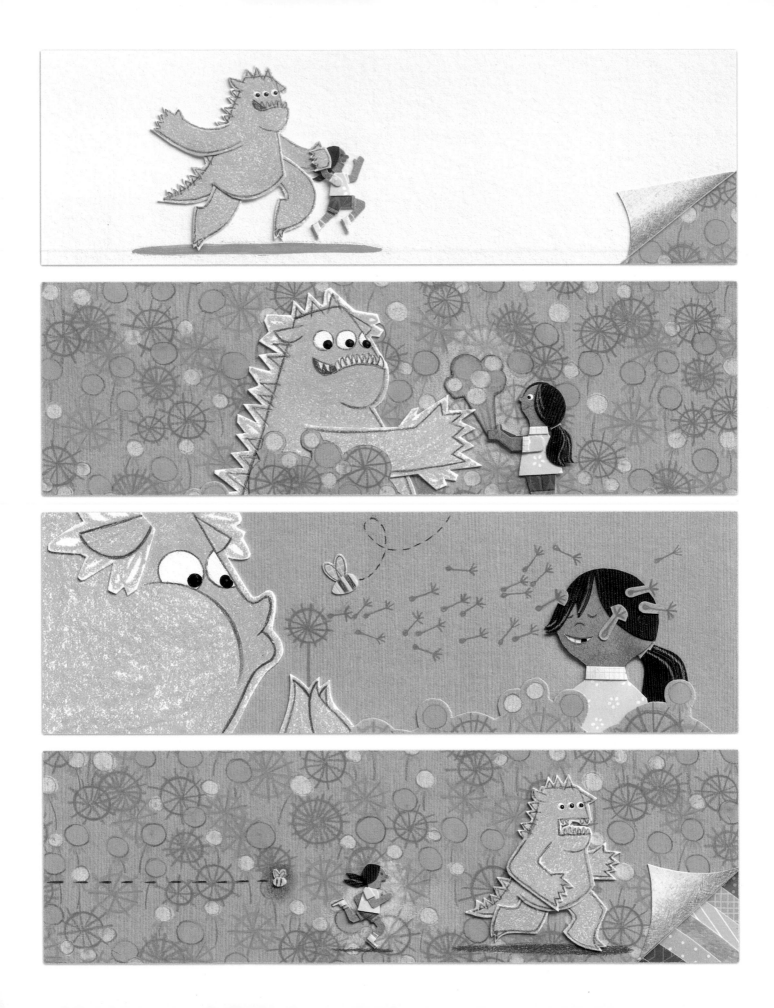

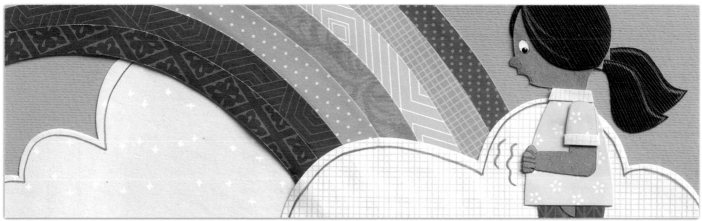